CW00841116

Table of Contents

Chapter 1: Introduction

The savannah was vast and seemingly endless, stretching as far as the eye could see. The grass was tall and golden, swaying gently in the warm breeze. Here and there, trees dotted the landscape, offering shade to the animals that roamed beneath them.

It was a place of wonder and magic, a place where the laws of nature held sway. The animals that lived there were wild and free, each one unique and special in their own way. There were zebras, their black and white stripes blending together in a mesmerizing pattern. There were giraffes, with their impossibly long necks and delicate features. And there were elephants, their massive bodies swaying as they made their way through the grasslands.

But of all the animals that called the savannah home, none was as mighty as the lion. He was the king of the jungle, his golden mane flowing in the wind as he strode through the tall grass. His roar could be heard for miles around, striking fear into the hearts of all who heard it.

One day, as the lion was out for a walk, he came across a small mouse. She was scurrying along the ground, her tiny legs carrying her as fast as they could go. The lion stopped in his tracks, curious about this little creature that seemed so insignificant compared to him.

"Hello there," he said, his voice deep and rumbling. "What are you doing out here all alone?"

The mouse stopped and looked up at the lion, her eyes wide with fear. She knew that lions were dangerous creatures, capable of killing with a single swipe of their powerful claws.

"I'm just looking for food," she said, her voice trembling.

The lion cocked his head to one side, studying the mouse with interest. He had never really noticed how small she was before, but now that he looked at her more closely, he could see that she was indeed very tiny.

"Well, be careful," he said. "There are many dangers out here on the savannah. You never know what might be lurking around the next corner."

The mouse nodded, grateful for the lion's warning. She scurried away as fast as she could, her heart beating wildly in her chest.

But little did she know that she would soon be back in the lion's company, and that their encounter would change both of their lives forever.

Chapter 2: The Lion's Predicament

As the sun began to set on the savannah, the mighty lion wandered through the tall grasses, looking for his next meal. His powerful muscles rippled under his tawny fur, and his amber eyes scanned the landscape for any sign of prey. Suddenly, he spotted a herd of gazelles in the distance, grazing peacefully. The lion crouched low, ready to pounce.

But as he bounded towards the gazelles, he didn't notice the hunter's trap hidden in the grass. With a loud snap, the trap closed around his paw, and the lion roared in pain and anger. He tried to break free, using all his strength, but the trap held firm.

For hours, the lion struggled to free himself. He roared and snarled, pulling with all his might, but the trap only tightened around his paw. The sun began to rise again, and the lion realized he was trapped for good.

He lay there, exhausted and defeated, his head resting on his paws. As the hours passed, he watched the other animals of the savannah go about their business, oblivious to his plight. He felt ashamed and embarrassed to be trapped like this, unable to escape.

But then he heard a tiny voice calling out to him. "Are you okay?" it said. The lion looked up and saw a small mouse peering up at him, its beady eyes filled with concern.

The lion snorted in disbelief. What could a tiny mouse possibly do to help him? But the mouse was undeterred. It scampered up onto the lion's paw and began to gnaw at the ropes of the trap.

At first, the lion barely noticed. But as the mouse continued to chew, he began to feel a glimmer of hope. Maybe, just maybe, the mouse could help him escape.

With renewed energy, the lion began to pull at the trap again, straining against the ropes. And with a sudden snap, he was free! He roared in triumph, thanking the mouse for its help.

From that day on, the lion knew that even the smallest creatures could make a big difference. And he never forgot the lesson he had learned, that true strength comes not just from physical power, but also from the help of others, no matter how small or unlikely they may seem.

Chapter 3: The Mouse's Help

As the lion's roar echoed across the savannah, it caught the attention of a small, curious mouse. Intrigued, the mouse scampered over to the source of the noise to investigate.

Upon arriving, the mouse found the mighty lion caught in a hunter's trap, struggling to free himself. The mouse watched as the lion used all his strength to break free, but to no avail.

Determined to help the lion, the mouse approached him and offered her assistance. At first, the lion scoffed at the mouse's offer, thinking that her tiny size would make her useless in helping him escape. However, the mouse was not deterred and insisted that she could help in some way.

The mouse surveyed the trap carefully, looking for any weaknesses or points of weakness that she could exploit. After a few moments, she noticed that the ropes binding the trap together were frayed and worn.

The mouse got to work, gnawing away at the ropes with her sharp teeth. Despite her small size, the mouse's determination was admirable, and she gnawed away tirelessly at the ropes until they finally gave way.

With the ropes cut, the trap was rendered useless, and the lion was able to break free. The lion was astonished by the mouse's bravery and resourcefulness, and he thanked her for her help.

The little mouse simply shrugged and said that it was no big deal, but the lion knew better. He realized that even the smallest creatures can make a big difference, and he was grateful for the mouse's help.

As the two unlikely friends stood side by side, they marveled at the lessons they had learned. The lion learned that even the mightiest of creatures can be humbled, and the mouse learned that her size didn't matter when it came to helping others.

Together, the lion and the mouse continued their journey through the savannah, inspired by the kindness and bravery they had shown each other.

Chapter 4: The Lion's Surprise

The mighty lion couldn't believe what was happening. He was caught in a hunter's trap, his paw tightly snared by the metal teeth of the trap. He roared with all his might, hoping that someone, anyone, would hear him and come to his aid.

As fate would have it, a brave little mouse happened to be nearby. She heard the lion's roar and, being curious and daring, decided to investigate. As she approached the trap, she could see the lion's massive form struggling to break free.

The mouse scurried closer, undaunted by the lion's intimidating size. "Do not be afraid," she said to the lion. "I can help you escape from this trap."

The lion was taken aback. He had always considered mice to be tiny, insignificant creatures, no match for his own strength and power. He couldn't imagine how a little mouse could possibly help him break free from the trap.

"Are you sure you can help me?" he asked the mouse skeptically.

"I am small, but I am clever and determined," the mouse replied. "Let me try."

The lion hesitated for a moment, but then decided to let the mouse have a chance. He watched as the mouse climbed up the side of the trap, her tiny claws digging into the metal. She reached the top and started gnawing at the ropes that held the trap shut.

The lion could hardly believe what he was seeing. The mouse was making quick work of the ropes, gnawing through them with her sharp little teeth. The lion was impressed by the mouse's tenacity and bravery. He realized that he had been wrong to underestimate her.

As the last rope snapped, the trap sprung open and the lion was free. He roared with joy and gratitude, thanking the mouse for her help.

"I cannot believe that a small creature like you could be so brave and strong," the lion said to the mouse. "You have taught me a valuable lesson today. I will never underestimate the power of the small and weak again."

The mouse smiled up at the lion, feeling proud and accomplished. She had shown that even the tiniest creatures can make a big difference in the world. As the lion and the mouse walked away, they knew that their unlikely friendship had just begun, and that they would always have each other's backs.

Chapter 5: The Mouse's Plan

The brave little mouse scampered up to the hunter's trap, her heart pounding with fear and determination. She knew that the mighty lion was trapped inside and needed her help to escape. She peered through the bars and saw the lion's massive paw ensnared in the thick rope, holding him tight.

The mouse knew that the rope was too thick for her to gnaw through, but she wasn't about to give up. She had to find a way to free the lion and save him from certain death. She scurried around the trap, looking for anything she could use to help her.

Suddenly, she spotted something glinting in the grass. It was a tiny pair of scissors, dropped by the hunter when he set the trap. The mouse's heart leaped with hope. She knew that if she could just get the scissors up to the top of the trap, she could cut the rope and free the lion.

With all her might, the little mouse began to climb the trap. The bars were slick with dew and the metal was cold against her paws, but she didn't give up. She climbed higher and higher until she reached the top, panting and exhausted.

She took the scissors in her tiny jaws and peered down at the lion. "Hold on tight," she called out, "I'm going to cut you free!" The lion looked up at her, amazed at her bravery. He had never seen a mouse so small and yet so fearless.

The mouse positioned the scissors carefully around the thick rope and began to saw. It was slow going, but she didn't give up. Inch by inch, the rope began to fray and loosen, until finally, with one final snip, the lion was free.

The lion stretched his massive limbs and roared with joy. "Thank you, little mouse!" he exclaimed. "You have saved my life!" The mouse beamed with pride, thrilled that she had been able to help the mighty lion.

The lion and the mouse made their way back to the savannah, where the other animals were waiting. They were amazed to see the lion walking beside the mouse, his massive head bowed in gratitude. The little mouse had done what no one thought was possible: she had saved the king of the savannah.

From that day on, the lion and the mouse were the best of friends. They roamed the savannah together, teaching the other animals the valuable lesson that even the smallest creatures can make a big difference. And the little mouse never forgot the thrill of climbing to the top of the trap and setting the mighty lion free.

Chapter 6: The Lion's Gratitude

The lion was amazed. He had always thought of himself as the most powerful and mighty animal in the savannah. But now, here he was, standing before a small mouse who had just saved his life. He looked down at the mouse, who was now standing at his feet, looking up at him with bright, curious eyes.

"You...you saved my life," the lion said, his voice filled with awe.

The mouse nodded, a small smile on her face. "Yes, I did," she said. "I couldn't just let you suffer in that trap."

The lion looked at the mouse for a long moment, his eyes taking in her small size and delicate features. He realized then that he had been wrong to judge her, and all other small creatures, based on their size. This little mouse had proven to him that even the smallest creatures can make a big difference.

"Thank you, little mouse," the lion said, his voice full of gratitude. "I never thought I would owe my life to a creature as small as you."

The mouse's smile grew wider. "It was my pleasure," she said. "I'm just glad I could help."

The lion thought for a moment, then looked back down at the mouse. "You know, little mouse," he said, "I may be a powerful and mighty lion, but I can never repay you for what you have done for me. However, I promise you this: I will always remember your kindness, and I will always be here for you if you ever need my help."

The mouse looked up at the lion, her eyes wide with surprise. She had never expected the powerful lion to be so kind and grateful. "Thank you," she said softly. "That means a lot to me."

From that moment on, the lion and the mouse became unlikely friends. They would often be seen walking through the savannah together, the lion towering over the little mouse. But despite their size difference, they were equals in every other way. They had learned that everyone has something to offer, no matter how big or small they may be.

As they walked, the lion would often pause to look down at the mouse and smile. He knew that he had learned a valuable lesson from her, one that he would never forget. The lesson that even the smallest creatures can make a big difference, and that true strength comes not from physical power, but from kindness, bravery, and gratitude.

And so, the lion and the mouse lived happily ever after, their friendship a shining example to all the animals of the savannah. They had proven that anything was possible, as long as you had the courage to believe in yourself and the kindness to help others.

Chapter 7: Conclusion

As the sun began to set on the vast savannah, the lion and the mouse sat side by side, enjoying the warmth of the fading rays. They had been through so much together, and now, they had become the most unlikely of friends.

The other animals of the savannah looked on in amazement. They had never seen a lion and a mouse together, let alone getting along so well. For so long, they had been taught to fear the lion and disregard the mouse. But now, they had learned a valuable lesson: everyone has something to contribute, no matter their size or strength.

The lion, with his mighty roar and powerful paws, had always been the king of the savannah. He had ruled over the other animals, and they had looked up to him with fear and respect. But when he found himself trapped in the hunter's snare, he was reminded that even the mightiest of creatures can find themselves in need of help.

It was then that the brave little mouse appeared, offering to help the lion escape. The lion had been skeptical at first, but the mouse had proven her bravery and resourcefulness. She had climbed up to the top of the trap and chewed through the ropes, setting the lion free.

From that moment on, the lion and the mouse had formed an unlikely bond. They had shared many adventures together, and the lion had come to appreciate the mouse's courage and loyalty. And in turn, the mouse had learned that even the most fearsome creatures can have a soft side.

As the other animals watched the lion and the mouse together, they began to see things differently. They realized that they had all been too quick to judge each other based on their size and strength. They saw the value in the little mouse's bravery, and they saw the kindness in the lion's heart.

And so, as the sun set on the savannah, the lion and the mouse remained together, happy in each other's company. The other animals looked on with newfound respect and admiration. They had learned a valuable lesson, one that they would never forget: everyone has something to contribute, no matter how small or mighty they may seem.

Chapter 8: Moral of the Story

"The Lion and the Mouse" is a fable that teaches an important lesson about the value of kindness, bravery, and gratitude. The moral of the story is that even the smallest and seemingly weakest creatures can make a big difference in the world.

In the story, the brave little mouse shows compassion for the mighty lion when he is trapped and in need of help. Despite the lion's initial skepticism, the mouse proves that her small size and lack of strength do not define her worth. She is able to free the lion and save his life.

The lion, in turn, learns the importance of gratitude and promises to repay the mouse for her kindness someday. Through this act of kindness, the lion also learns that everyone has something to offer, no matter their size or strength.

This lesson is important for children to learn because it teaches them to treat everyone with kindness and respect, regardless of how they may appear on the surface. It encourages children to look beyond the exterior and to appreciate the unique strengths and qualities of others.

Furthermore, the fable highlights the value of bravery in the face of adversity. The mouse could have easily been intimidated by the powerful lion, but she chose to act with courage and determination in order to help him. This bravery paid off in the end and allowed her to make a significant impact in the world.

Lastly, the fable emphasizes the importance of gratitude. The lion recognizes the mouse's bravery and kindness and promises to repay her someday. This shows children the value of acknowledging and appreciating the good deeds of others. Gratitude fosters positive relationships and creates a sense of community, which is essential for a healthy and happy society.

In conclusion, "The Lion and the Mouse" is a heartwarming fable that teaches children important lessons about kindness, bravery, and gratitude. It encourages children to see beyond the surface and to appreciate the unique qualities of others, to act with courage and determination in the face of adversity, and to express gratitude for the good deeds of others. These are valuable lessons that will serve children well as they grow and interact with the world around them.

Printed in Great Britain
by Amazon